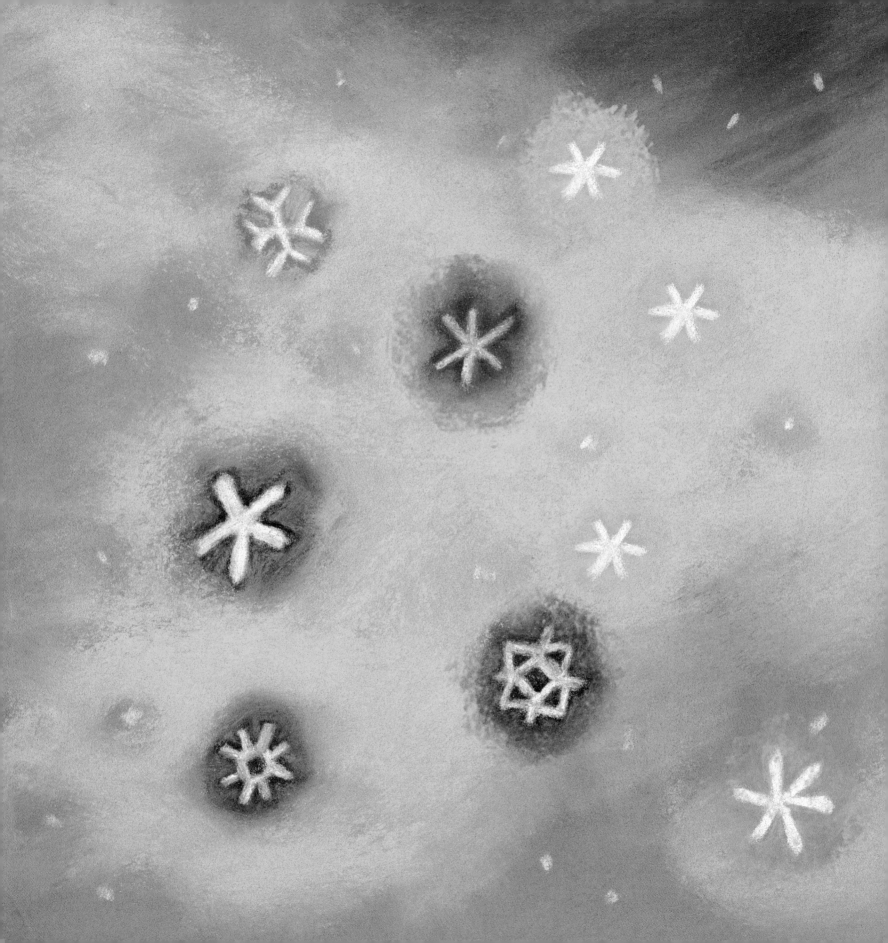

For Alexander and Thomas — G.S.

For Sossy and Phil — R.R.

First published 2008 by Macmillan Children's Books
This edition published 2011 by Macmillan Children's Books
a division of Macmillan Publishers Limited
20 New Wharf Road, London N1 9RR
Basingstoke and Oxford
Associated companies throughout the world
www.panmacmillan.com

ISBN: 978-1-4472-0270-7

Text copyright © Gillian Shields 2008
Illustrations copyright © Rosie Reeve 2008
Moral rights asserted.

1 3 5 7 9 8 6 4 2

A CIP catalogue record for this book is available from the British Library.

Printed in China

Gillian Shields

Sam's Snowflake

Illustrated by Rosie Reeve

MACMILLAN CHILDREN'S BOOKS

It was Christmas Eve, and Sam felt very excited.
Dad was setting off to the forest, to fetch
a special Christmas surprise.

"Don't be long!" said Sam, giving him a big bear hug. "I'll be back as soon as the first flakes of snow start to fall," smiled Dad.

Sam couldn't wait for the snow to come.

Every Christmas, Dad helped him
to make a snow bear,

took him
tobogganing

and played roly-poly
snowball fights.

"When will Dad get home?"
Sam sighed.

"Don't worry," laughed Mum.
"Dad will be here soon,
and so will the snow."

"Come and help me with these
honey cakes while we're waiting."

So Sam helped Mum to make
cakes and biscuits and
puddings and pies.

Everything smelled
warm and spicy.

But Dad still wasn't back —
and there was no snow.

"Let's put up the decorations," said Mum. "That will help to pass the time."

So Sam helped Mum to arrange big branches of holly and silver fir cones and red berries. Everything glowed and shone.

But Dad still wasn't back — and there was no snow.

"We mustn't forget to wrap the presents for our friends," said Mum. So Sam helped to make a big pile of coloured parcels.

But Dad *still* wasn't back — and there was not a single flake of snow.

Sam looked out of the window.
Outside, it was cold and dull and dark.

Perhaps Dad, and the snow, would need
some help finding their way.
Sam had an idea!

He found some paper and glitter and cotton wool.
Then he was busy for a long time, while Mum roasted some
chestnuts over the fire. At last, Sam said, "Look! It's ready!"

It was Sam's snowflake!

"If I put this in the window, the snow will find our house,"
Sam said happily. "And so will Dad," he whispered.

It was getting late.
Sam stuck the snowflake high in the window
and Mum hung up his stocking.

"Time to go to sleep, Sam," she said.
"Dad should be here when you wake up."

"I do hope so," thought Sam,
as he snuggled under
the blankets.

Sam's snowflake shone in the window.
Outside, high in the dark sky,
a single star burned brightly.
At last, Sam yawned and blinked
and fell asleep.

Out in the forest, Dad was still far from home. He walked along slowly, pulling something heavy behind him. He looked up and sniffed the air. "Snow's on the way," Dad grunted. "Sam will be pleased."

Before long, the wild winter weather swirled through the forest, blocking the paths and darkening the sky. But in the distance, Sam's snowflake shone out bravely, like a star.

Sam woke up.
It was Christmas!

There were presents in
his stocking, and lovely
smells of special food
drifted up the stairs.

Through the window,
there was a new, white
world, covered in snow.

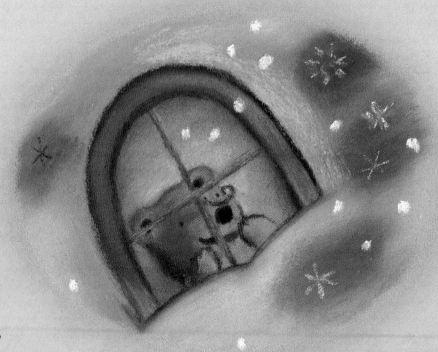

But,

But,

BUT . . .

Sam's heart sank.
There was still no Dad.

Christmas just wouldn't be the same
without Dad. Sam started to cry.
He tore down his paper snowflake
and threw it out of the window.

"It didn't work," he muttered.
"*It didn't work.*"

Just then, a quick cold breath of wind caught the snowflake.

and fluttered . . .

It danced . . .

and floated . . .

down to the garden . . .

. . . where Someone was putting the finishing
touches to a special Christmas surprise.

"Come and look at the snow, Sam," called Mum.
Sam dried his eyes, put on his scarf
and trudged outside.

And there was the biggest surprise of all!
"You **DID** arrive with the snow, Dad!" shouted Sam,
and he gave Dad the best of bear hugs.

"I think this belongs to you," said Dad, holding the
little paper snowflake that winked and blinked like a star.
"Thank you for guiding me home, son."

Sam had the happiest
Christmas ever, playing
in the snow with Dad,

as hundreds of little snowflakes danced and glittered for Christmas Day.

But the brightest
one of all . . .

. . . was Sam's snowflake,
shining at the top of Sam's tree.

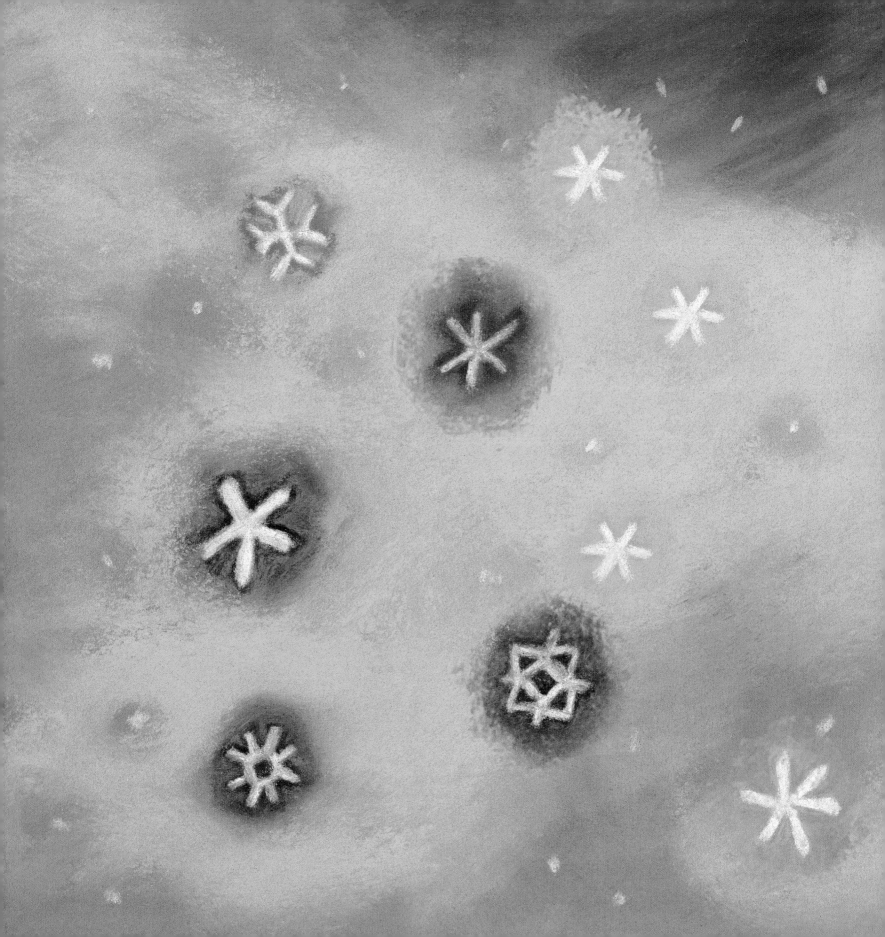

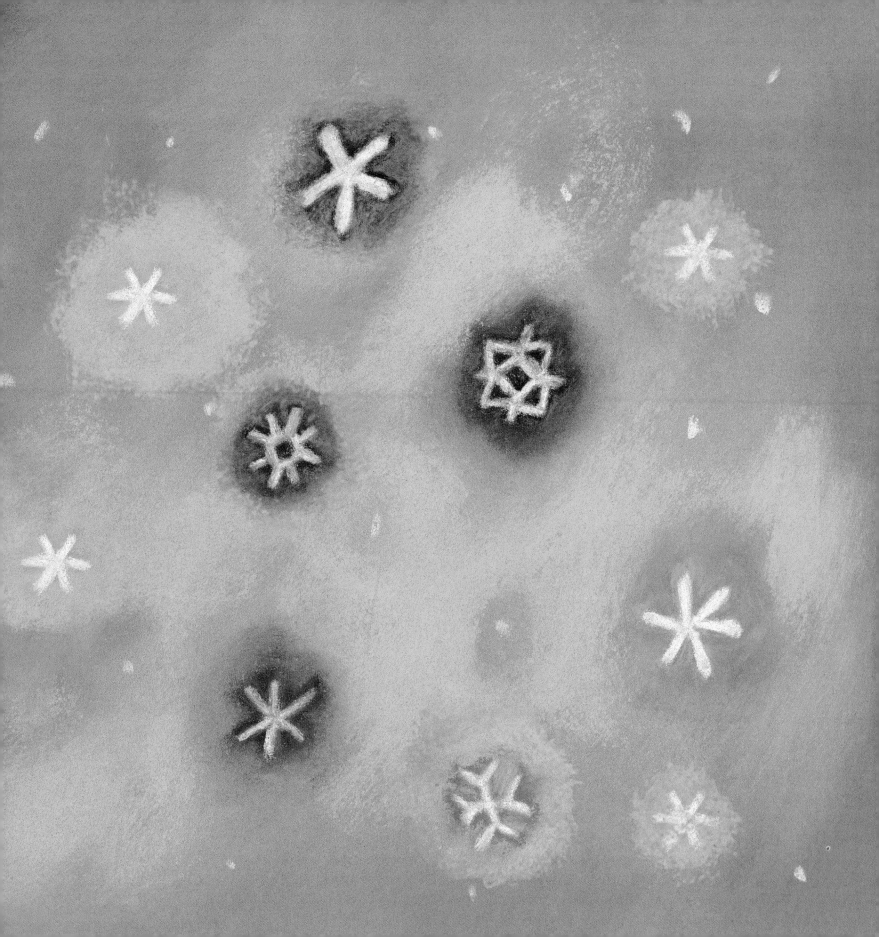